Our Puppy's Holiday

For John, Martina, Sophie and Gemma Aston –
and Paddy

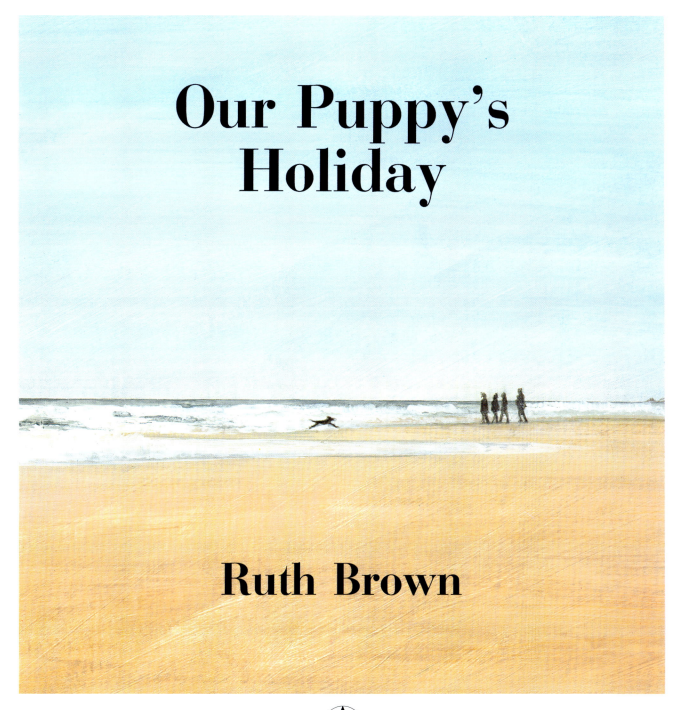

Our Puppy's
Holiday

Ruth Brown

Andersen Press · London

It was our puppy's first holiday.

Everything was new to her:
the wide, wide beach,

the screeching gulls

and the crashing waves.

She played hide-and-seek

and follow my leader

and leap-frog

and another game of hide-and-seek,

this time with a difference!

There were new things to eat

and drink!

There were hills to climb

and walls to climb.

But an old tree was a problem

in more ways than one.

She made friends – sometimes easily

sometimes not so easily.

She was having such a good time

that she just wanted to go on playing

and playing

even in the dark!

For she didn't know – that it was only the first day!

Andersen Press paperback picture books

THE PICNIC
by Ruth Brown

IT AT FIRST YOU DO NOT SEE
by Ruth Brown

THE TALE OF GEORGIE GRUB
by Jeanne Willis & Margaret Chamberlain

THE TALE OF MUCKY MABEL
by Jeanne Willis & Margaret Chamberlain

SCRUMPY
by Elizabeth Dale & Frédéric Joos

I HATE MY TEDDY BEAR
by David McKee

THE MONSTER AND THE TEDDY BEAR
by David McKee

THE HILL AND THE ROCK
by David McKee

MR UNDERBED
by Chris Riddell

MICHAEL
by Tony Bradman and Tony Ross